SESAME STREET

3-Minute Stories

  publications international, ltd.

sesameworkshop™

The nonprofit educational organization
behind Sesame Street and so much more
www.sesameworkshop.org

Published by
Louis Weber, C.E.O., Publications International, Ltd.
7373 North Cicero Avenue, Lincolnwood, Illinois 60712

Ground Floor, 59 Gloucester Place, London W1U 8JJ

Customer Service: 1-800-595-8484 or customer_service@pilbooks.com

www.pilbooks.com

p i kids is a registered trademark of Publications International, Ltd.

8 7 6 5 4 3 2 1

ISBN-13: 978-1-4127-3782-1
ISBN-10: 1-4127-3782-6

CONTENTS

Elmo and Oscar

Written by Gayla Amaral
Illustrated by DiCicco Studios

It was a gorgeous day for games on Sesame Street, but Elmo couldn't find any playmates.

"Who will play with Elmo?" said the furry little monster. "Maybe Oscar!"

Clang! Clang!

Elmo knocked on Oscar's trash can.

"Pretty-please come out and play," the furry little monster begged.

Oscar poked his grouchy head out of the can and asked, "You talkin' to me? Well, I don't want to play. Now scram!"

Elmo was not surprised, since Oscar was often a little grouchy. But Elmo wasn't going to give up.

"Maybe if Elmo makes him an anchovy milk shake, Oscar won't be so grouchy," Elmo thought. "Maybe then he'll want to play."

Elmo raced off to make a shake, then …

Bang! Bang!

Elmo knocked on the trash can once again and offered Oscar the slimy shake. Oscar grabbed the milk shake — and slammed his lid shut.

"Why won't Oscar play?" sighed Elmo.
Suddenly, Elmo had an idea. Oscar liked rainy days.
Maybe he would play if he thought
it was raining.
So Elmo
hurried home
and got a
watering can.

"It's raining, it's pouring," Elmo sang, dripping water on Oscar's trash can. But Oscar didn't fall for it.

"Maybe Oscar will come out to see his little old grandma," Elmo thought. So Elmo draped a blanket over his red fur and wore a grandmotherly cap.

Tap! Tap!

Elmo knocked on the can. In a sweet voice he called, "Oh, Oscar dear. Will you please come play with Grandma?"

Oscar raised the lid, letting out a smelly whiff of sardine-and-donut casserole.

"Oh, it's you again," Oscar replied. "Not a bad trick, but it didn't work! Read my lips: no, no, no!"

Elmo still wasn't ready to give up. There must be *some* way to change Oscar's mind. Elmo thought and thought and thought.

"Elmo needs to think some more," he sighed, then smiled. "Elmo's got it! Elmo will pretend to be a garbageman! Then Oscar will be glad to come out and play."

In a deep, gruff voice, Elmo called, "Garbageman here to pick up the trash!"

Oscar *loved* trash. He wasn't about to give any away.

"I keep all my trash for my junk collection," Oscar snapped. "Wait a minute!" he continued, recognizing Elmo. "Trying again, eh? I'm beginning to like you. And I don't like *that!*"

With that, Oscar slammed the lid and disappeared into his can.

Elmo was willing to try again to come up with a terrific idea. If Oscar wouldn't play with Elmo or a grandma or a garbageman, who *would* Oscar play with?

Then Elmo remembered that his mommy had just gotten a brand-new trash can.

"Elmo knows!" Elmo shouted. "Maybe Oscar will play with a *grouch!*"

Elmo rolled his trash can right next to Oscar's. Elmo lifted the lid and climbed inside.

Clunk! Clunk!

Knocking his can against Oscar's, Elmo growled in his best grumpy voice, "Another grouch here to play with Oscar!"

Oscar's head shot up! Of course, he soon saw it was Elmo in the other can. Oscar couldn't help but admire Elmo's clever idea.

"You win, fuzzface," said Oscar. "What do you want to play?"

Elmo knew just the game.

"Let's play… Grouches!"

Grover's One-Man Band
(Part 1)

Written by Elizabeth Clasing
Illustrated by Joe Ewers and DiCicco Studios

One of Elmo's favorite things to hear was, "Are you ready for a story?" Elmo thought those were some of the best words in the world. So when the librarian asked that question, Elmo got excited.

"YES!" he shouted, along with all the other little monsters in the Sesame Street Library.

"Yes, *please*," Elmo added. He was a very polite monster. "Elmo would love to hear a story."

The nice librarian monster smiled at everyone in the circle. "Today's story is about a friend of yours," she told them. "A cute, furry blue monster named…"

"Grover?" Elmo guessed. And he was right!

"Yes, this is a story about Grover and his search for some marvelous music," said Marian, the librarian.

"Oh, goody," Elmo said. He liked stories about his friends on Sesame Street best.

Marian opened the book and began....

One day, Grover was strolling down Sesame Street when a big poster caught his eye.

"Oh my goodness, a 'Sesame Street Jamboree,'" Grover read out loud. "I cannot believe it! A jamboree right here on Sesame Street. How exciting!"

He called over to Big Bird, who was just bouncing down the steps of 123 Sesame Street.

"Um, Big Bird," said Grover. "Can you tell me, what is a jamboree?"

Big Bird smiled. "Why, it's just a great big festival, like a party, with lots of music and…"

"MUSIC?" Grover cried. "But I *love* music. I must be in the Jamboree, too!"

"Anybody can be in it. You just need to make music somehow," said Big Bird. He tapped his chest feathers proudly. "I'm going to march and sing."

"Something to make music, *hmmm?*" Grover said. "I will get started on that right away."

Grover headed straight home and asked his mommy for something that made music. She reminded him about the banjo Uncle Schlomo had given Grover for his birthday last year.

As Grover's mommy spoke, a playful breeze rustled the curtain at the window. It also tickled the wind chime hanging there. The soft ringing sound made Grover stop and stare.

"Aha!" Grover shouted.

Grover arrived at the playground a little while later with his banjo. The wind chimes were tied to the top and jingled as he walked.

Some friends were in the park, too. A bunch of them were bopping a funny conga dance behind Ernie, who was playing an old harmonica.

"That is just what I need to make even *more* music," Grover said wistfully when he saw it.

"Here you go, Grover." Ernie handed it over with a grin. "It's yours! I have another one at home I can use that's even noisier. Just ask Bert."

Grover thanked Ernie before skipping back to Sesame Street. He was practicing a screechy little tune when Oscar popped out of his can.

"What's that noise?" Oscar wondered. "I love it!"

Oscar was so impressed with Grover's music, he lent the blue monster a beat-up bicycle bell and two old trash can lids.

Grover was making up a new little song for his musical collection when he saw something wonderful in the window of a shop nearby.

"What a cute, adorable monster," Grover said, smiling at himself in the shiny glass.

Then he noticed the horn.

Luckily, Grover's friend Ruthie owned the shop. She was happy to let Grover borrow the horn.

As Grover walked away, he gently strummed his banjo—***throom***—rattled his wind chimes—***ling***—hummed his harmonica—*zmmm*—clanged the trash can lids—***krish***—rang his bell—*ching*—and even blew his own horn—***whaaa***.

"No doubt about it," he said, sighing happily. "I, Grover, am one very, *very* musical monster."

Ernie's Space Adventure

Written by Guy Davis
Illustrated by DiCicco Studios

"It's beddy-bye time," said Ernie with a yawn. Rubber Duckie made a tiny little squeak.

Ernie looked down at his favorite toy. "What's that, Rubber Duckie? You're not tired?"

Just then, Ernie's buddy, Bert, let out a loud snore.

"Well, it sure sounds like *somebody* is tired," Ernie grinned. "Okay, Rubber Duckie, if you promise to keep real quiet, we'll stay up for a little while."

He looked out the window at the starry night as he gave Rubber Duckie a little pat.

Quietly, Ernie whispered
his favorite nighttime rhyme:

Star light, star bright,
First star I see tonight,
I wish I may, I wish I might,
Have the wish I wish tonight.

Then he stared at the moon
as he settled upon his pillow.
"I wonder what it's
like up there," thought
Ernie as his eyes slid
closed. "I wish
I could fly
to the moon
someday."

Just as he was drifting off to sleep, Ernie's eyes opened wide. What was he thinking? This was no time for sleeping. His rocket ship was about to take off . . . . Wait, what rocket?

"Ten seconds to liftoff!" came an announcement. "Nine, eight, seven . . . ."

Ernie looked around. He and Rubber Duckie were astronauts in a rocket—and about to fly into space! Was he dreaming?

". . . six, five, four . . ."

"No time to worry about that now," thought Ernie.

". . . three, two, one, *BLAST OFF!*"

"Here we go, Rubber Duckie!" Ernie shouted. "We're on our way to the stars!"

Rubber Duckie squeaked in reply.

"I don't care if I'm dreaming or not," answered Ernie. "This is incredible!"

The rocket blasted into space,
leaving Earth far behind.
Everywhere Ernie looked
there were beautiful
stars, blazing
comets, and
amazing
planets.

Ernie and Rubber Duckie raced around the solar system, seeing all its wonders.

"There's only one thing that would make this trip better," said Ernie, "and that's if my ol' buddy Bert were here, too."

As their rocket zoomed close to the moon, Rubber Duckie made a sound.

"You want to check out the moon?" Ernie asked him.

Rubber Duckie squeaked a "yes-I-would-like-to-check-out-the-moon" kind of squeak.

So Ernie landed their rocket. They strapped on their astronaut helmets and hopped down onto the moon's surface.

"Yoo-hoo, anybody here?" yelled Ernie. Then he gasped. Walking toward him was an alien! It looked very familiar, only Ernie didn't know anyone with an extra set of eyes growing out of his head, a lizard-like tail, and webbed hands and feet.

"Welcome to the moon!" said the alien. Rubber Duckie squeaked a surprised hello.

"Honka womp womp hoyer," said the alien. "Derosa warble rezza gleet gleet vanderlaan!"

Ernie didn't understand the alien's squeaky language, but it seemed to make sense to Rubber Duckie.

"What's that Rubber Duckie?" Ernie asked. "He said that I look familiar? Tell him that's funny, because he looks familiar too. But I'm not sure why that is."

Rubber Duckie squeaked Ernie's reply to the alien as Ernie smiled and extended a hand to his new friend. Ernie began to giggle as the two shook hands. The alien's webbed fingers tickled! Ernie laughed even harder.

"Ernie, wake up!" Ernie opened his eyes. Suddenly, he wasn't on the moon anymore. He was in his own bed, with Bert shaking him awake.

"Ernie, that must've been *some* dream!" grumbled Bert. "You were laughing so loud you woke me up."

"Sorry about that, Bert!" smiled Ernie. "But a dream like that comes along once in a blue moon!"

Nighttime Zoo

Written by Gayla Amaral
Illustrated by DiCicco Studios

Elmo was so excited! He was going to the zoo. "Elmo will see great big elephants and lions and tigers and monkeys!" he said enthusiastically.

When he arrived, Elmo met a friendly zookeeper who knew all about animals. Elmo had lots of questions. "What do elephants eat? Why do zebras have stripes? Which animal is the smartest?"

"Those are great questions," laughed the zookeeper as they walked through the zoo. Suddenly Elmo stopped. Something was different in this part of the zoo. Elmo tried to figure out what it was.

"Why is it so quiet? Where are the animals?" he asked curiously. There were no animal sounds—no monkeys chattering and no tigers growling.

"Look up in the tree. *Hoo-hoo* do you see?" chuckled the zookeeper.

Elmo looked up. "Elmo sees an owl, but he's asleep. Is he taking a nap?" he whispered.

The smiling zookeeper explained that owls sleep during the day because they stay awake all night. She explained that animals that do that are called nocturnal animals.

Elmo looked around and saw more animals sleeping right in the middle of the day!

"Do those opossums and raccoons stay up all night, too?" Elmo wondered. He thought it would be nice for the owl to have some friends at night.

The zookeeper nodded. "That's why they're all called nocturnal animals. It means that they mostly come out at night."

Elmo imagined the moon and stars shining in the sky as the animals played and looked for a midnight snack. But then he thought of one little problem. "How do they see?" he wondered aloud. "Elmo would need a flashlight at night, but opossums and raccoons don't use those."

"Good question, Elmo," the zookeeper responded. "They have special eyes to help them see in the dark."

Elmo wondered what it would be like to stay up all night long. It would be fun to stay up past bedtime every night!

The clever zookeeper guessed just what Elmo was thinking.

"So, would you like to be a nocturnal monster, Elmo?" she teased.

"Yes!" Elmo answered. "Elmo wants to be a nighttime monster and see in the dark to play with Zoe, Big Bird, and Elmo's other friends."

Just then, something occurred to Elmo.

"Uh-oh!" exclaimed Elmo, as he remembered his friends. "If Elmo had special nighttime eyes, Elmo would be lonely without his friends." Not only that, Elmo thought, he wouldn't be able to see the sunshine or a rainbow.

Elmo decided it was neat that there were animals out at night, but that it wasn't the life for him. "Not Elmo!" he said loudly.

Elmo didn't realize how loudly he was talking. Suddenly, he heard the owl call, *"Hoo-hoo!"*

"Me! Me!" giggled Elmo. "Elmo's sorry that he woke you up, Mr. Owl," he said. The owl ruffled its feathers and flapped its great big wings.

"I wonder how we can help the owl fall asleep again," said the zookeeper. "He needs his rest."

Elmo had a great idea. "Elmo can tell the owl a bedtime story!" he exclaimed.

"Once upon a time, there was a little nighttime monster named Elmo," he began. Elmo continued his story about a monster that awoke every night at dark and fell asleep every morning when the sun came up. Just as Elmo finished his story he saw that the owl's eyes had closed again.

But someone else had fallen asleep, too. "Nighty-night, Owl," Elmo whispered. "Nighty-night, Zookeeper."

Hats Off to Big Bird

Written by Guy Davis
Illustrated by Bob Berry

It was a lazy afternoon on Sesame Street and Big Bird was feeling a bit lazy himself. He decided that a nap was in order, so he settled into his comfy nest. In no time, Big Bird was fast asleep and dreaming a funny dream.

"Hello there, Big Bird," said Grover. "I, your furry pal Grover, am happy to join you in this dream to present you with a collection of hats."

In the dream, Big Bird smiled at Grover and his large pile of hats. "I bet there's a hat for everyone on Sesame Street!"

"You are rootin' tootin' right, partner," drawled Grover, who was suddenly wearing a cowboy hat. "There is a new sheriff on Sesame Street, and his name is Sheriff Grover!"

"Oh gosh, I like using my imagination," replied Big Bird. "I want to try on something, too. I'll wear a helmet and imagine that I'm a brave firefighter!"

"Howdy there, Firefighter Big Bird," said Sheriff Grover. "You are a very **BIG,** brave firefighter, just like I am a very **CUTE,** blue sheriff!"

Big Bird's dream next took him into space ... with another furry friend! "Oh, hello, Elmo," Big Bird said dreamily. "Which hat do you like best?"

"Oh, Elmo likes the astronaut's helmet," said Astronaut Elmo. "Elmo is pretending to be an astronaut in space. Elmo is using his imagination."

Big Bird's imagination was working overtime in his funny dream, too. Because the next thing he knew, he dreamed he was in the Count's castle.

"Which hat would you like to wear, Count?" Big Bird asked.

The Count chose the green hat with the little daisy.

Big Bird wondered why.

"Because then I can count all the daisy petals," laughed the Count. "One petal…two petals…three, four, five petals…six petals! Ah-aa-aa-ah!"

Big Bird laughed with him and wasn't a bit surprised when Rosita appeared in his crazy dream.

"*¡Hola!*" said Rosita. "I would like to pick a hat, too! I want to be queen for a day!"

"Good choice, Rosita," agreed Big Bird. "You look very queenly in that crown!"

What a fun dream! All of Big Bird's best friends were in it.

The dream wasn't over—before Big Bird woke up there were more friends to visit.

"You'd better wear this hat, Bert," said Big Bird, handing him a blue and green bicycle helmet.

"Whoa!" Bert shouted, wobbling down the road.

"I'm glad he's wearing that hat," said Big Bird to himself.

Before he knew it, Big Bird was handing out hats to even more friends. He gave a knit cap to Ernie to wear outside, and he gave a puffy white chef's hat to Cookie Monster.

"So me can bake all kinds of snacks!" said Cookie.

That's when Big Bird woke up. He smiled and told himself, "There really is a hat for everyone on Sesame Street." But then he remembered one friend who wasn't in his funny dream. He climbed out of his nest and went to find her.

"Zoe! Wait until you hear about my nap and my dream about hats," Big Bird said when he found Zoe. She was getting ready for a nap of her own.

Big Bird told her all about it.

"I'm sorry I didn't give *you* a hat," he said.

Zoe giggled. "That's okay, Big Bird. Maybe *I'll* have a dream about hats…and I'll try them all!"

Someone to Play with Grover

Written by Guy Davis
Illustrated by DiCicco Studios

Hello, everybody! This is your furry pal, Grover. I am in my playroom, and I am looking for someone to play with me.

As you know, I, your old pal, Grover, make a very good playmate. First of all, I am cute and furry, and everyone knows cute and furry monsters make wonderful playmates.

Perhaps you would like to play with this pretty-pretty red balloon? Did you know that balloons pop very, very easily? Maybe there is something else we can play with that does not go *POP!*

We can save this red balloon for later.

Look what I found! I, your helpful toy-box guide, Grover, have discovered a toy chest filled with many things that will surely provide us with hours of fun!

What? You say it is a lovely day for playing outdoors? That is a very smart observation.

I have an excellent idea. We can pretend we are explorers digging for dinosaurs. Now I, your lovable explorer, Grover, will show you how to dig... *puff, puff...* and dig... *puff, puff!* Hmmm ... I am having a teensy bit of trouble. I did not know that digging for dinosaurs is such hard work.

I am sure we have dug a hole halfway to China.

Sweet maracas! If we dig all the way to China, it will take a very long time to walk back home to Sesame Street. We will probably get home after dark, and then we will not be able to play anymore! What kind of playmate would Grover be then?

I think that is enough digging for now! Let us move on to something else.

Oh! Oh! I know. Just to show you what a wonderful playmate I can be, I shall show you a skill of mine. I, Grover, will juggle three balls in the air—all at once—while balancing a pail of water on my head. Stand back! I, Grover, am now ready to begin.

Many of you may think this is easy, but I assure you, this is a very difficult stunt... *OW! OW! OW!*

Okay, that was not such a good idea. So I am going to try this with *two* balls and a pail of water on my head... *OW! OW!*

Okay, maybe I will juggle just one ball in the air while still balancing the water bucket on my head! Watch as I begin juggling this one colorful rubber ball... *OW!*

Hmmm... I am having a teensy bit of trouble with juggling, too.

Luckily, we still have the pretty-pretty red balloon. My, I did not realize it was such a BIG balloon. Oh, dear. This pretty balloon is taking me up, up, and away! Hmmm…it is **REALLY HIGH** up here. Sesame Street looks **REALLY SMALL!** How will I ever get down? Perhaps one of these pretty birds will help.

POP!

Okay, playtime is over. Thank you for playing with your furry pal, Grover. I hope you will join me, the adorable Grover, again tomorrow. And that you will remember that balloons pop very, very easily. Good-bye! Whew.

Elmo's Music Box

Written by Gayla Amaral
Illustrated by DiCicco Studios

Elmo was feeling a little blue for no reason that he knew. "Elmo doesn't feel very happy," he sighed.

"Why don't you listen to some music, Elmo?" suggested his mommy. "Music makes *me* feel happy."

Elmo's face lit up as he picked up his favorite music box. As the music played, Elmo leaped to his feet and began dancing.

"Elmo feels very happy now!" he said cheerfully, as he danced out the door and down Sesame Street with his music box in hand. Soon he saw Rosita.

"*Hola,* Elmo," said Rosita sadly. "You look so happy. I wish I were happy, too." Rosita explained that her grandmother had gone to a salsa dance class, so Rosita couldn't visit her *abuela.*

"Elmo will make
you happy," he said,
winding his music box. The cheerful music soon had
Rosita tapping her feet and clapping to the sound.

"*¡Gracias, amigo!* I feel much happier now!"
exclaimed Rosita, hugging her friend. "This music
box is wonderful!"

Suddenly, Elmo felt something big and shaggy jump on him, covering him with great big sloppy kisses. It was Barkley!

"Stop, Barkley!" giggled Elmo. But the lovable dog kept licking his face happily. Elmo was still laughing when he heard a voice.

"Barkley, what has gotten into you?" exclaimed Betty Lou. "I'm so sorry, Elmo. I don't know why Barkley ran off like that."

Betty Lou explained that Barkley had been sad because he couldn't find the spot where he'd buried his bone. She thought it might cheer him up to go for a walk in the park, but nothing seemed to make him happy until they saw Elmo.

"Elmo's music made Elmo feel happy. And it made Rosita happy, too. Maybe Elmo's music made Barkley feel better," suggested the little red monster.

Dancing with his friends took a lot of energy, so it wasn't long before Elmo's happy feeling turned into a hungry feeling. He knew just what he needed: a snack from Hooper's Store. When Elmo reached the store, he saw Cookie Monster with a plate of cookies and a big glass of milk.

"Hi, Cookie Monster," said Elmo. But Cookie Monster barely looked at Elmo. "What's wrong?" Elmo asked. "Does your tummy hurt? That's a lot of cookies!"

"Me tummy okay," replied Cookie Monster. "But me not happy. Me have too many cookies and no one to share."

Poor Cookie Monster! He was just lonely.

Elmo knew just what to do. He picked up his trusty music box, wound it up again, and let the music play. Soon Cookie Monster was tapping his toes and humming along.

"That nice song," said a more cheerful Cookie. "Hey! Me have idea. Me share cookies with you and me munch to the music!"

Cookie Monster handed Elmo a cookie, just as Rosita danced into the store.

"That's a happy dance," said Elmo.

"My *abuela* taught it to me," Rosita replied. "She learned it in her salsa class. It makes me happy because it reminds me that I'll visit her very soon!"

Soon Barkley came running through the door with Betty Lou holding tightly to his leash. Barkley clutched a great big bone in his mouth as he danced excitedly around Elmo.

"Look, Elmo," said Betty Lou. "Barkley found his missing bone. And I think he wants to thank you for cheering him up with your music box."

"You're welcome, Barkley," giggled Elmo. "And Elmo is glad you found your special bone."

Then Cookie Monster shared his cookies so that everyone could have a snack.

Elmo looked at his music box with a smile.
"Elmo is happy, and Elmo's friends are happy,"
said the little red monster. "Music and sharing make
everybody happy—even doggies!"

Cookie's Monster

Written by Catherine McCafferty
Illustrated by DiCicco Studios

Cookie Monster was baking monster-chip cookies, his favorite treat. Monster chips are really raisins.

"One monster-chip cookie, two monster-chip cookies, three monster-chip cookies, four monster-chip cookies, five monster-chip cookies, six monster-chip cookies, seven monster-chip cookies!" Cookie Monster thought for a minute. "Me eat one now, and one just after now. And then all the rest monster-chip cookies!" Cookie Monster said. *Chomp, Chomp!* Down two cookies went. He couldn't wait to eat the rest!

Someone else couldn't wait, either. Elmo was walking by Cookie Monster's door when he smelled something delicious. Elmo peeked through the kitchen door into Cookie Monster's kitchen.

"Knock, knock!" called Elmo.

"Who there?" asked Cookie Monster.

"Elmo!"

"Elmo who?" joked Cookie Monster.

"Elmo loves cookies!" said Elmo.

"Then Elmo come in!" Cookie Monster opened the door. "Me have plenty monster-chip cookies to share!"

"Oh, Cookie Monster, Elmo loves monster-chip cookies!" said Elmo.

"Monster-chip cookies very special cookies. Me only make them for sometimes treat. Recipe handed down from Cookie Monster Mommy to Cookie Monster," said Cookie Monster. Elmo ate every last crumb of his yummy monster-chip cookie.

"Could Elmo have one to take for Elmo's mommy?" he asked.

Cookie Monster nodded, but he was a little worried. There were only five monster-chip cookies left.

"Maybe me eat one now," said Cookie Monster. But before he could take a bite, someone else peeked in the window.

"Knock, knock!" called a voice.

"Who there?" called Cookie Monster.

"Zoe, Zoe, Zoe!" said Zoe.

"Zoe, Zoe, Zoe who?" asked Cookie Monster.

"Zoe, Zoe, Zoe wants to visit Elmo and Cookie Monster and taste yummy-smelling cookies!" Zoe answered back.

Cookie Monster opened his door once again.

"Hello, Cookie Monster. Hello, Elmo," said Zoe. "Can I have a cookie?"

"Yes, can Zoe have a cookie?" Elmo asked Cookie Monster. Cookie Monster gulped. But Zoe asked so nicely he couldn't refuse. He even let Elmo wear his baking hat.

"Now Elmo can help Cookie Monster bake cookies," Elmo giggled. "Well, Elmo can help *eat* the cookies."

Zoe munched a cookie while Elmo pretended to be a baker.

Meanwhile, Cookie Monster counted his cookies. There were only two left! And suddenly, there were two new faces at his door.

"Hey, Bert," said Ernie. "Do you smell cookies?"

"Why, yes, Ernie. I think they are Cookie Monster's special monster-chip cookies," said Bert.

Cookie's Monster

"Knock, knock!" said Ernie.

"Who there?" asked Cookie Monster.

"Bert," said Bert.

"And Ernie," said Ernie.

"Bert and Ernie who?" asked Cookie Monster.

"Bert and Ernie who would really like to taste your monster-chip cookies," laughed Ernie.

Cookie Monster let in Bert and Ernie and sadly handed them the last two cookies.

Zoe, Bert, and Ernie chomped on their delicious monster-chip cookies. Cookie Monster could only look at his empty plate. "Me made monster-chip cookies," thought Cookie Monster. "And me made Cookie Monsters out of friends!"

Just then, the oven's buzzer went off.

Buzz! Buzz!

"What that?" said Cookie Monster.

"No, no," said Elmo. "Cookie Monster should say, 'Who's there?'"

"Oooh, I like this game, I like this game!" clapped Zoe excitedly.

The alarm buzzed again.

Buzz! Buzz!

"Who there?" said Cookie Monster.

The oven didn't answer, so Elmo did.

"Cookie?" he said.

Then Cookie Monster remembered. He'd baked a second batch!

"Cookie!" He hurried to open the oven door.

"Cookie who?" asked all of his friends.

"More monster-chip cookies, that who!" said a very happy Cookie Monster. "Enough for friends…and enough for Cookie Monster!"

Zoe's Silly Secret

Written by Guy Davis
Illustrated by DiCicco Studios

Elmo and Zoe were outside during playtime at preschool, when a little birdie's chirping made Elmo giggle. Suddenly Zoe made an announcement.

"I know a silly secret!" said Zoe excitedly.

"What is it?" asked Elmo. "What secret does Zoe know that Elmo doesn't?"

"It's a secret *about* Elmo!" giggled Zoe as she played with the barrettes in her hair. "You have to guess!"

"Elmo likes guessing secrets," said Elmo. "Tell Elmo a clue, Zoe, please?"

"Okay, I will give you a clue," said Zoe. She leaned close to Elmo's ear. "Are you ready?"

"Elmo is ready," said Elmo, giggling because Zoe's whispering tickled his ear.

"The secret is … I know Elmo's very favorite thing!" said Zoe.

"Elmo's favorite thing? That's easy," replied Elmo. "Elmo's favorite thing is playing with Zoe!"

"Nope, that's not the secret thing!" laughed Zoe as she ran away. "You think about it."

Elmo decided to follow Zoe down the block to pick up some more clues. He spotted her talking to Oscar the Grouch and sneaked up to listen.

"Oscar, would you like to hear what Elmo's favorite thing is?" asked Zoe.

"Do I look like I want to hear what Elmo's favorite thing is?" grouched Oscar.

"Yes!" said Zoe brightly.

"Well, you would be wrong because I don't want to hear what Elmo's favorite thing is!" replied Oscar.

"Oh, Oscar, don't joke me!" laughed Zoe. "Let me whisper it to you!" Zoe whispered in Oscar's ear.

"Are you finished?" asked Oscar grumpily, hiding a smile. "Then … scram!"

"Okay, Oscar!" replied Zoe. "I'll see you later!"

Zoe skipped off … with Elmo following closely behind!

Zoe skipped back into preschool. Elmo slipped in behind her and spied Zoe talking to Grover.

"Grover, let me show you Elmo's favorite thing," said Zoe, writing on the chalkboard.

"I, your lovable pal, Grover, already know Elmo's favorite thing," said Grover. "Elmo likes it when I become the one, the only, Supergrover!"

"That's *one* of Elmo's favorite things," said Zoe. "Let me tell you Elmo's *most* favorite thing …."

Elmo couldn't stay quiet any longer.

"Wait, Zoe!" said Elmo. "Elmo knows the answer. Elmo's favorite thing is Elmo's pet goldfish, Dorothy."

"Nope, that's not it!" answered Zoe.

"Elmo's favorite thing is using Elmo's imagination!" said Elmo.

"Good guess, but that's not the secret!" said Zoe.

"Elmo's favorite thing is … mustard!" said Elmo.

Zoe's Silly Secret

"Don't joke me!" laughed Zoe as she put her hands on her hips. "Are you serious?"

Elmo fidgeted around a bit.

"Well, Elmo's running out of guesses," he said. "Can Elmo have some more clues?"

Zoe nodded and led Elmo and Grover outside.

Bert had found a feather in the playground and was using it to tickle his friends. Elmo laughed to see everyone—even Oscar—being tickled.

"That's the clue!" Zoe said.

"Oh, Elmo knows!" Elmo said excitedly. "The silly secret is that Elmo has *lots* of favorite things! Dorothy is Elmo's favorite fish, Oscar is Elmo's favorite grouch, and Supergrover is Elmo's favorite hero," he said. "And Elmo's favorite game is being tickled."

"Well, you do have lots and lots of favorite things, Elmo," said Zoe. "But that's not the secret. You have one *more* favorite thing!"

Elmo started giggling because now Zoe started tickling *him.*

"What is it?" giggled Elmo. "What favorite thing did Elmo forget?"

"Elmo loves to laugh!" shouted Zoe, and everyone giggled together.

Under the Bed

Written by Guy Davis
Illustrated by DiCicco Studios

Where, oh where can my teddy bear be?
Oh where, oh where can he be?
With his little brown eyes and his cute little tail,
Oh where, oh where can he be?

Grover was all ready for bed, but first he had to find his teddy bear.

"I am ready to go to sleep," said Grover. "I have brushed each and every one of my teeth, and I am wearing my very favorite polka-dotted pajamas. But even a furry, cute monster like me needs his teddy bear! Where can he be?"

So Grover looked high, and Grover looked low. Grover looked beside the nightstand and in his closet. In fact, Grover looked everywhere, except…

"Goodness!" gasped Grover. "What if my teddy bear is *under the bed?*"

Grover gulped a big gulp. "It is not as if I am afraid to look under the bed just because it is dark under there," he said to himself.

"No, I am not afraid of looking for Teddy under the bed," repeated Grover. "But even a furry, cute monster like myself might need some safety gear."

So Grover gathered a few items in case there were any problems while searching under the bed. As he collected the items, Grover hummed his little song:

Where, oh where can my teddy bear be?
Oh where, oh where can he be?
With his little brown eyes and his cute little tail,
Oh where, oh where can he be?

Finally, Grover was ready for his big adventure. He was wearing a scuba mask to protect his eyes and his bunny slippers to protect his feet.

"I, your furry pal Grover, always believe in being prepared," said Grover, "and that is why I have my flashlight and my butterfly net and my fishing pole."

Grover also grabbed a banana, just in case.

"It is time to go under the bed," announced Grover. He took a deep breath, lifted the blanket and sheets, and shined his flashlight under the bed.

"Oh my goodness!" gasped Grover. "What is *that?*" Something strange was staring right at him!

But after taking a closer look, Grover realized that he was looking at a dusty dinosaur toy.

Under the Bed

As he looked for his teddy bear, Grover spotted several things he had been missing.

"I wondered where those crayons were!" exclaimed Grover. "And look, here is my basketball!"

Just then, Grover froze. Something caught his eye. Slowly, Grover shined his light toward the dark shape.

"There you are, Teddy!" smiled Grover.

Grover grabbed his teddy bear and held him close.

"Even a brave monster like myself misses his teddy bear," said Grover. "I knew I would find you!"

"And as long as I am in this dark and dangerous place," thought Grover, "I will also rescue my other toys." He collected his crayons, ball, and dinosaur, and crawled out.

Later, after Grover snuggled into bed with his cuddly teddy bear, he sang his little song again:

Where, oh where can my teddy bear be?

Oh where, oh where can he be?

With his little brown eyes and his cute little tail,

Oh where, oh where can he be?

As Grover drifted off to sleep, he imagined he could hear his teddy bear whisper in reply, "I, Grover's teddy bear, am right here where I belong. Good night!"

Elmo's Fantasy Band

Written by Guy Davis
Illustrated by Tom Brannon and Bob Berry

Elmo was in the middle of a daydream. "Elmo loves music! Elmo loves music so much that someday Elmo will have his own band!" he said.

Zoe overheard Elmo and got very excited.

"Don't joke me!" said Zoe. "Will you really?"

"Yes, really!" said Elmo. "Elmo loves to sing and make music for everyone!"

"Elmo, can I be in your band, too?" asked Zoe.

"Elmo would love for Zoe to be in his band," said Elmo. "We can call it 'Elmo and Zoe's Band'! And Zoe can play keyboards!"

"Yay!" exclaimed Zoe, as she jumped up and down excitedly. "I love keyboards!"

Then she stopped bouncing.

"Um, what's keyboards, Elmo?" she asked. But Elmo didn't answer. He was too deep in his dream. "Elmo will ask Louie to play drums and Elmo will get Big Frankie to play guitar, too!"

In Elmo's daydream, Big Frankie and Louie were very excited about being in a band. Louie even did a little solo on his drum: *Boom-budda-boom-budda-BOOM! BOOM! BOOM!*

83

"Elmo knows just the place for our band to play," said Elmo out loud. "Elmo and Zoe's Band can play at the Sesame Street Talent Show!"

"Oh, Elmo," said Zoe, "I feel proud! Our band will play the bestest music ever!"

Now Zoe could imagine it, too: The band worked together to load instruments onto a bus headed for the show.

"Elmo knows the perfect song to sing right now," she imagined Elmo might say. "Everyone sing along!"

The wheels on the bus go round and round,
round and round, round and round.
The wheels on the bus go round and round,
all through the town!
The drums on the bus go boom-boom-boom,
boom-boom-boom, boom-boom-boom.
The drums on the bus go boom-boom-boom,
all through the town!

The guitars on the bus go strum-strum-strum,
  strum-strum-strum, strum-strum-strum.
The guitars on the bus go strum-strum-strum,
  all through the town!
The keyboards on the bus go plink-plink-plink,
  plink-plink-plink, plink-plink-plink.
The keyboards on the bus go plink-plink-plink,
  all through the town!

Elmo and Zoe's band arrived at the recreation center where the Talent Show was about to start. The stage crew helped them set up for the show.

"Hey, Elmo," said Big Frankie. "I'm a little nervous. I think I have stage fright!"

"Just try really hard, Big Frankie," said Elmo. "Think about how happy people will be when they hear our music!"

"No time to be nervous," growled Louie. "We have a show to do!" The band ran onstage.

"Welcome to the Sesame Street Talent Show!" Zoe yelled to the crowd. "Are you ready to sing along?"

"Here's one of Elmo's favorite songs," added Elmo. "It sounds a little like 'Old MacDonald.' Everyone sing along."

"Let's kick it!" said Zoe, dancing around the stage. In the dream, Elmo and Zoe asked everyone to sing….

Elmo and Zoe had a band, M-U-S-I-C!
And in that band, they played all day, M-U-S-I-C!
With a BOOM-BOOM here,
And a BOOM-BOOM there.
Here a BOOM, there a BOOM,
Everywhere a BOOM-BOOM!
Elmo and Zoe had a band, M-U-S-I-C!
Now everybody clap along, M-U-S-I-C!
With a CLING-CLANG here,
And a CLING-CLANG there.
Here a CLING, there a CLANG,
Everywhere a CLING-CLANG!
Elmo and Zoe had a band, M-U-S-I-C!
And in that band, they played so well, M-U-S-I-C!
With a BING-BANG here,
And a BING-BANG there.

Here a BING, there a BANG,
  Everywhere a BING-BANG!
Elmo and Zoe had a band, M-U-S-I-C!
  M-U-S-I-Ceeeeee!

"Thank you!
G'night!"

Winter into Spring

Written by Catherine McCafferty
Illustrated by Bob Berry

What a wonderful winter day! Telly Monster certainly thought so. He glided through the falling snow on ice skates. He practiced forward skating, backward skating, and even loop-de-loops!

Telly skated round and round the pond as the snow stopped and a wintery sun peeked out. "Skating is my favorite sport next to bouncing on pogo sticks," said Telly to himself, "even though I can't skate in triangles." Telly skated another loop-de-loop.

Seeing the snow stop made Telly think about the day when winter would be over. No more snow. No more ice. No more ice-skating! "What will I do then?" he worried.

Telly skated in slower and slower circles and finally stopped skating. He realized that the ice wouldn't last forever. Soon winter would end.

"Hi, Telly!" Elmo waved from the edge of the pond. Telly glided sadly over to Elmo.

"Oh, Telly is a great skater! Elmo really loves to watch Telly!" Elmo clapped but it didn't cheer up Telly Monster.

"Thank you, Elmo," said Telly with a sad sigh.

"Why is Telly sad?" asked Elmo.

"Winter is going to end, and we won't be able to skate." Telly sighed again.

"No more winter?" asked Elmo sadly. "But Elmo loves winter!"

"Oh, no, I knew this would happen," said Telly. "Now you're sad, too." Elmo tried to think of something to cheer them both up. "But something good happens when winter ends," he said.

"It does?" asked Telly.

Elmo nodded. "Spring!"

"But I love *winter!*" said Telly.

Elmo thought for a minute. "But Telly likes colors too," he said.

Telly nodded. "I *love* colors!"

"Spring is full of colors!" Elmo said. "Remember? There are rainbows in spring."

"Even Oscar smiles when he sees one," Telly said.

Elmo giggled. He remembered something else springy. "Bert's kite was all different colors, too. Do you remember? The one he flew last spring!"

"I changed my mind," said Telly. "I don't mind if winter ends. I love spring!" But then ...

"Oh, no, but then spring will end, too," he groaned.

"When spring ends, summer starts," said Elmo.

Telly still didn't look very happy, so Elmo went on.

"Remember? Elmo and Telly had lots of fun last summer at the Count's soccer game. Elmo remembers Telly cheering!"

"Yes, yes, I remember!" Telly bounced up and down on his skates.

"After the game, we did yo-yo tricks!" Telly added.

Telly had almost forgotten about his yo-yo! Where was his yo-yo, anyway? Telly was just starting to worry about *that* when Elmo tugged his hand.

"Telly, Telly!" said Elmo. "Hurry, hurry!"

Telly looked around. What happened? "What's wrong, Elmo?" he asked.

"Nothing's wrong, Telly," said Elmo. He glided onto the ice with Telly. "Elmo wants to have winter fun to remember in summer!"

"Okay Elmo," said Telly. After all, when winter ended, a wonderful new season would start. Skating with his friend, Telly's worries melted away … like snow.

Elmo's Wonderful Day

Written by Elizabeth Clasing
Illustrated by Tom Brannon and DiCicco Studios

Hello, it's Elmo. Elmo wants to tell you all about his day. But first, tell Elmo: What did *you* do today? Did you learn something new? Did you play a game? Did you help somebody? Did you run and jump and spin? Elmo hopes so!

Elmo had a *wonderful* day. Do you want to hear about it? You do? Hooray!

Elmo's day started with the best dream ever. Elmo was dreaming about a merry-go-round. Elmo's horsie came to life and ran away to Sesame Street. It even jumped over Oscar's can. Silly horsie!

Oh, Elmo almost forgot. Elmo is supposed to be telling you about his wonderful day!

When Elmo woke up, there was no merry-go-round. But there was a big, yellowy sun outside the window. Elmo knew he had to run right out and play. Do you ever feel like that on a sunny day? You *do?*

Can you guess who was waiting to play? Elmo will give you a hint. She was wearing a tutu.

Did you guess Zoe? You are so smart. Zoe and Elmo played Skip-to-My-Lou for a while. Some of Elmo's other friends danced with us, too.

Elmo played another game next. It starts with a song.

Do you know where to find your nose? Can you touch your toes? Then you can play.

It goes like this:

"Head, shoulders, knees and toes, knees
Head, shoulders, knees and toes, knees an

Oh, you know that game, too?

Today, Elmo played it with Zoe, but Elm
silly. Elmo made up new words.

Why don't we play it together RIGHT N
Elmo will start out not-so-silly.

"Head, shoulders, knees and toes, knees
Head, shoulders, knees and toes, knees an

Okay, ready to play Elmo's way? Hooray!

"Ears, elbows, belly button, belly butto

Ha ha, hee hee! Belly button! That's Elm
part! Do it again.

"Ears, elbows, belly button, belly butto

Wow, you sure are good at this game.

After we played Elmo's favorite game, we played Zoe's favorite, too. That made Zoe feel happy. Guess what? Making Zoe feel happy made *Elmo* feel happy.

Zoe really likes pretending, so we played that. Zoe likes pretending she is a barrelina....

Oops! Elmo means *ballerina*. Ballerina! Ballerina! Can you say ballerina? It makes Elmo's mouth all twisty to say that. You try it. Try really hard!

Elmo and Zoe pretended to be ballerinas together. Having a tutu helps Zoe pretend. Elmo wishes he had a tutu, too, but Elmo can pretend without one.

Zoe told Elmo to spin around like a ballerina. So Elmo did.

Elmo went so fast around and around, Elmo got dizzy and **BOOM!** Elmo fell on the grass with his tummy feeling all tickly.

We laughed and laughed!

Tickle your tummy and you'll see. **Ha ha hee hee!**

Elmo's wonderful day was not over yet! There were still some more games to play.

Elmo showed Zoe how to jump rope. Up. Down. Up. Down. Up. Down.

Zoe's toes got all mixed up at first. They went down instead of up. Sometimes even dancers need a friend to help them learn something new.

Elmo likes to help. So Elmo helped Zoe. And Zoe jumped all the way to ten. Now Elmo knows: Ballerinas are *very* good at jumping.

Then Zoe showed Elmo another way to jump. We hopped in a game named hobscotch. Uh-oh! Oops again! Elmo means *hopscotch*. Elmo had to count all the way to ten to play. Count with Elmo.

One. Two. Three. That's good! Say the next part really *fast*: fourfivesix. Elmo has a little trouble with the next part, so now go slow: seven…eight…nine.

Elmo's Wonderful Day

Okay. Say the last part really, really *loud:* TEN!

Ha ha. That was fun!

Elmo and Zoe played hopscotch all the way home.

See, Elmo said it was a wonderful day.

Grover's One-Man Band
(Part 2)

Written by Elizabeth Clasing
Illustrated by Joe Ewers and DiCicco Studios

What story would you like to hear today?" asked Marian, the librarian.

Elmo and his friends shouted out ideas.

"Goodnight Moon!" "Puss in Boots!" "A story about refrigerators!"

No one could seem to agree.

"Can we hear another story about Grover and his one-man band?" Elmo asked. "Elmo really liked the last one about him."

All the other little monsters cheered that idea.

"I think there was more to that story," said Marian. "Remember, Grover had a banjo…"

"It went *throom!*" said a blue monster.

Marian nodded. "Yes, and he had a wind chime and harmonica," she said.

"Ling! Zmmm!" yelled another monster.

"And some trash can lids and a bicycle bell came next," said Marian.

"Krish! Ching!" two monsters said together.

"And a horn that went *whaaa*," added Elmo.

Marian opened her book. "Right. Now, here is how the story ends," she said.

No one could believe their eyes. Grover had just arrived in the park where some friends were practicing for the Sesame Street Jamboree.

Grover noticed their surprise and nodded. "I *know*. I could not believe it myself. Why would someone throw away a perfectly good tuba?"

Grover had spotted the big horn in the trash behind Moe's Music Store when he stopped to talk to Cookie Monster on the way to the park.

Bert gasped in wonder. "Grover! Are you going to play *all* those instruments?"

Grover blushed proudly. "Yes. My mommy will be so proud when she sees me in the Jamboree. I will be the most musical monster there."

Prairie Dawn gave Grover a tambourine she had put aside. "I'm not using this, Grover," she said.

Grover's eyes opened wide with delight. "Oh, goody! You know, there is even *more* music out there. And I am off to find it!"

He ran off, clinking, clanking, and hooting all the way.

But the Jamboree was almost ready to start and Grover had already found quite a bit of the music there was to be found. He had a banjo from Uncle Schlomo and his mommy's wind chimes. He had Ernie's old harmonica, plus Oscar's beat-up bicycle bell and two noisy trash can lids.

That's not all! Grover had borrowed Ruthie's horn, and now he carried a great big tuba and Prairie Dawn's tambourine, too.

What else was left?

Just then a bouncy, squeaky song drifted past his ear. *Week week week.*

Grover followed the squeaking song to Ernie and Bert's apartment. Bert was home from the park and he looked surprised to see Grover again, especially when Grover walked right past him.

"Where are you going?" Bert cried. "Grover!"

But Grover was already asking Ernie if he could borrow one more thing. It was yellow and, at the moment, squeaky-clean.

"Sure, Grover," Ernie said. "But only if I can come, too! I'll even bring my bubbles."

"Oh, Ernie," Bert sighed.

Music was already filling the block when Grover stepped through the doors of 123 Sesame Street.

"That is the sound of a jamboree just waiting for ME!" Grover cried. He tucked Rubber Duckie, his last music-maker, inside the tuba. Then he began strumming, squeaking, humming, honking, and marching along.

Everywhere along the street, people came out to see what was making all the racket.

There were balloons flying, honkers bouncing, birds singing, and even Ernie blowing bubbles.

But what made everybody laugh and join in the Jamboree was the sound coming from Grover.

"Elmo thinks that's the best music ever," said Elmo to Oscar. For once, Oscar agreed.

The clanging, rattling, and ringing of all those instruments was music to a Grouch's ears.

"He's a regular one-man band," said Oscar.

Elmo giggled and clapped for his friend. "No, Grover is a one-*monster* band...and adorable, too!"

Big Bird: Photographer

Written by Gayla Amaral
Illustrated by DiCicco Studios

Big Bird was thrilled with his new camera and photo album. They were gifts from Maria and Luis.

"Maybe I'll take pictures of things I see on Sesame Street," the feathered photographer thought as he made his way down the block, taking lots of photos.

"Oh, no! I only have *five* pictures left," sighed Big Bird. "What should I photograph next?"

When he saw Bert and Ernie walking his way, he had an idea. "I know what I'll do," he exclaimed. "I'll take pictures of all my friends!"

"May I take your picture?" Big Bird asked. His friends happily agreed and Bert smiled at the camera.

"Say cheese," said Big Bird.

"Ern-nieee!" cried Bert, shaking his head when he saw the picture.

Next, Big Bird took a picture of Cookie Monster. "Say cheese," said Big Bird.

Of course, Cookie Monster said "Cookie!" instead.

"I have *one* picture of Bert and Ernie and *one* picture of Cookie Monster," counted Big Bird. "That's *two* pictures, so I have *three* more left."

"Maybe I'll take a photo of Oscar," said Big Bird. He was sure that even a Grouch would like having his picture taken.

Big Bird knocked on Oscar's trash can.

Clang! Clang!

"Hi, Oscar," said Big Bird as the Grouch peeked out from his trash can. "Can I please take your picture for my photo album?"

"No, you cannot!" grumbled Oscar, slamming the lid down. But Big Bird didn't give up.

Clang! Clang! Big Bird knocked again. Oscar raised the lid. "Oh, it's you again. Don't you understand what no means? No means no!"

But before Oscar could slam the lid shut, Big Bird aimed his camera. "Say cheese, Oscar!"

"Scram!" growled the green Grouch instead. But it was too late.

Now Big Bird had *one* picture of Bert and Ernie, *one* picture of Cookie Monster, and *one* picture of Oscar. That added up to *three* pictures, so there were *two* more left to take.

"Gosh, who will be my next subject?" wondered Big Bird. "Grover would look great in my album." So Big Bird hurried off to find him.

"Would you let me take your picture?" Big Bird asked Grover.

"Be right with you," Grover said. He ran over to the wall and took down a picture of a puppy. "Ummm … is this the one you wanted?"

Big Bird couldn't help laughing. "No, Grover. What I mean is, will you let me take your photo with my brand-new camera?"

"Oh, now I see," said Grover. "Of course. Everyone should have a picture of a cute monster like myself."

Big Bird agreed and suggested that Grover act silly.

"No problemo!" responded Grover. "I, your cute lovable pal, Grover, will create the silliest photo you have ever seen."

And the furry, blue monster flipped upside down. Big Bird started to giggle as Grover began walking across the floor with his hands in his shoes and his gloves on his feet. Big Bird only stopped laughing long enough to tell him, "Say cheese, Grover!"

Instead, Grover proudly exclaimed, *"Voila!"*

Big Bird placed Grover's photo in the album and began to count.

"There's *one* picture of Bert and Ernie, *one* picture of Cookie Monster, *one* picture of Oscar, and *one* silly picture of Grover. I have *four* pictures. That means I have *one* picture left to take," said Big Bird. "It should be someone very special."

"That is a very good and astute observation," agreed Grover. "But who?"

Big Bird and Grover thought and thought. They both agreed someone special was missing from the photo album.

"I've got it! I, your furry pal Grover, will take a picture of *you,* Big Bird!" Grover exclaimed, grabbing the camera from his big, yellow friend.

"Say cheese, Big Bird," Grover said, as he snapped the picture.

"Cheese!" shouted Big Bird happily, grinning for the camera.

Big Bird placed his photo in the album next to the silly one of cute and adorable Grover.

"One, two, three, four, five," Big Bird counted proudly. *"Five* photos of funny friends."

Grover

Me

Sing-Along

Written by Elizabeth Clasing & Brooke Zimmerman
Illustrated by DiCicco Studios

The sun had set on Sesame Street, and the stars were starting to shine. It was time for all good little boys, girls, and monsters to go to bed.

Elmo was tucked in already, all snug and warm in his bed.

"Did you brush your teeth, Elmo?" Daddy asked, as he kissed Elmo good night.

Elmo nodded sleepily. And as his mommy started to sing a lullaby, Elmo's eyes slowly slid shut.

At first, it sounded like a lullaby Elmo knew by heart. But then he realized this was a special song.

Tonight, Mommy was singing with words made up just for him.

"Lullaby, kiss good night
   in the glow of a night-light.
Lie down, sleepyhead,
   in Elmo's soft bed.
Close your eyes now and rest,
   like a bird in its nest.
Close your eyes now and rest.
   Elmo, you are loved best."

The next morning, Elmo woke up humming the same little tune. As he washed his face, he chanted, "Lullaby, kiss good night." As he ate his oatmeal, he sang, "Lie down, sleepyhead." And when he hopped down the steps of 123 Sesame Street, he found himself serenading Oscar: "You are loved best!"

"Ewww," Oscar grumbled, slamming down his lid.

Elmo sighed. He loved his mommy's lullaby song, but the soft nighttime sounds didn't seem to fit with the bright daytime sun.

That's when Elmo saw Ernie and Bert, out for a walk with Bert's pigeon, Bernice.

"Hey!" shouted Elmo. "Hey, Ernie! Hey, Bert! Hey, pigeon! Elmo has to ask you something."

"Gee, Elmo," said Ernie. "It sounds sort of important."

"Oh, it is," said Elmo. "Very important. Elmo wants you to tell him how to get a lullaby out of Elmo's ears."

"Something's in your ears?" said Bert. "They look fine to me. Wait, did you say a *lullaby?*"

Elmo giggled. Then he explained, "Elmo's mommy sang a lullaby last night. Elmo loves it! But now it is stuck in Elmo's ears for good."

Ernie understood. "That's like *my* favorite song, 'Rubber Duckie,'" he said. He sang a bit, snapping his fingers. "I mostly sing it when I'm in the tub."

"Elmo knew you could help," Elmo said. "So what does Ernie do to get 'Rubber Duckie' out of his ears?"

Ernie thought for just a second. "That's easy, Elmo. I sing something else," he said.

"You know, Ernie, that just may work," said Bert.

"But what should Elmo sing instead?" Elmo asked.

"Bernice's favorite song is 'Mary Had a Little Lamb,'" Bert suggested. "What about that?"

Elmo smiled happily. "Elmo knows that one!" So Elmo started to sing: "Mary had a little lamb…" Then he stopped. "Elmo has an idea! Elmo will make up new words, just like Mommy did."

Elmo started again. His new song was so good, Ernie and Bert made him sing it again and again. In the end, they all sang it together. You can sing it, too!

Elmo has a lullaby, lullaby, lullaby,
    Elmo has a lullaby stuck inside both ears.
Everywhere that Elmo goes, Elmo goes, Elmo goes,
    Everywhere that Elmo goes,
That's all that Elmo hears!

Say Good Night, Ernie

Written by Guy Davis
Illustrated by DiCicco Studios

RINGGGGG!

"Ernie, turn off that alarm clock," said Bert. "It's bedtime, not time to get up!"

"I set the alarm clock so that I wouldn't forget to brush my teeth, Bert!" said Ernie, shutting off the noisy alarm. "You wouldn't want me to forget to brush my teeth, now, would you, Bert?"

"No, Ernie, I wouldn't want you to forget to brush your teeth," replied Bert. "Now get some sleep."

"Okay, Bert," Ernie said after brushing his teeth, "time for beddy-bye. The last thing I want to do is disturb my buddy Bert."

A few minutes later, Bert was sleeping peacefully.
RINGGGGG!

"Ernie, stop waking me up!" said Bert. "That is the loudest alarm clock I have ever heard!"

"I set the alarm clock so that I wouldn't forget to kiss Rubber Duckie good night, Bert!" said Ernie, shutting off the alarm clock. "You wouldn't want me to forget to kiss Rubber Duckie good night, now, would you, Bert?"

"No, Ernie, I wouldn't want you to forget to kiss Rubber Duckie good night," replied Bert, a little grumpily. "Now get some sleep."

"You got it, Bert," said Ernie. "The last thing I want to do is disturb my buddy Bert."

"Harrumph," said Bert. A few minutes later, Bert was sleeping peacefully.

RINGGGGG!

"Ernieeee!" cried Bert. "What could it possibly be now?"

"I set the alarm clock so that I wouldn't forget to take off my slippers, Bert!" said Ernie, shutting off the alarm. "You wouldn't want me to forget to take off my slippers, now, would you, Bert?"

"No, Ernie, I wouldn't want you to forget to take off your slippers," replied Bert, a little bit more grumpily. "Now go to sleep!"

"No problem, Bert," said Ernie. "The last thing I want to do is disturb my buddy Bert."

Bert mumbled something grouchy. A few minutes later, Bert was sleeping soundly.

RINGGGGG!

"ERNIE!" cried Bert. "What else do you possibly need to do before bed?"

"I set the alarm clock so that I wouldn't forget to put my glass of water next to the bed, Bert!" said Ernie. "You wouldn't want me to forget to put my glass of water next to the bed, now, would you, Bert?"

"No, Ernie, I wouldn't want you to forget to put your glass of water next to the bed," replied Bert, a *lot* more grumpily. This was becoming too much for him. "Now get some sleep."

RINGGGGG!

Say Good Night, Ernie

"Ernie, dare I ask?" groaned Bert.

"I set the alarm clock so that I wouldn't forget to read a bedtime story to help me fall asleep, Bert!" said Ernie, shutting off the alarm clock. "You wouldn't want me to forget to read a bedtime story now, would you, Bert?"

"No, Ernie, I wouldn't want you to forget to read a bedtime story," replied Bert, staring at the ceiling. "Now, please, can we get some sleep?"

"Will do, Bert," said Ernie. "The last thing I want to do is disturb my buddy Bert."

Bert buried his head in the pillow. A few minutes later, he was snoring softly.

RINGGGGG!

"Ernie," said Bert weakly, "this is getting ridiculous. Why is your alarm clock ringing again?"

"I think you should guess, Bert," said Ernie.

"NO, Ernie, I don't think I should guess," replied Bert.

"Oh sure you do, Bert," said Ernie. "Come on and guess, Bert."

Bert glared at Ernie.

"Come on, Bert," said Ernie. "Take a guess."

"Ernie, that's it!" cried Bert. "Stop right now and tell me why you set the alarm clock."

"Sorry,
Bert. You know
I don't want to
bother you," said Ernie,
shutting off the alarm
clock. "I set the alarm so that I
wouldn't forget to tell you good night, Bert! So…
good night, Bert!"

Bert smiled at his forgetful friend. "Good night,
Ernie," said Bert. "Sleep tight!"

Bubble Trouble

Written by Elizabeth Clasing
Illustrated by Maggie Swanson and DiCicco Studios

Night was falling when Big Bird tucked in his teddy bear and said, "I bet you'd like to hear a bedtime story before you go to sleep, Radar."

Big Bird pulled a book from his shelf. It was the same storybook that Luis used to read to Big Bird every night when he was a littler bird. It was one of his favorite stories because it was about Big Bird's friends. He knew it by heart.

"Here we go," Big Bird said....

"What's going on here?" Bert asked Elmo as the little red monster passed by. Bert blinked. Elmo wasn't walking by. He was *floating*.

"Wheee!" Elmo shouted joyfully as he drifted past.

Bert chased after him. "Who's making all these bubbles?" Bert asked Elmo.

"Nobody knows," Elmo answered.

Bert looked around at the mess. "Well, I'm going to find out!" he announced.

Elmo's bubble popped and plopped Elmo on the sidewalk beside Bert. "Elmo will help!" Elmo said.

Together the friends followed a stream of bubbles across to Grover's Restaurant. "Maybe they came from there," Elmo said to Bert, and he rushed inside.

Everything in the restaurant was super-slippery. There were suds in the salad and soap in the soup.

"One bologna sandwich coming up!" yelled Grover. "Um…make that one bologna-and-*bubble* sandwich."

Elmo waded over to ask chef Cookie Monster if the bubbles were coming from his kitchen.

"Uh-uh," Cookie Monster said, shaking his head. "No bubbles in kitchen. Only COOOOOKIES!"

Elmo went back to tell Bert that they were no closer to an answer. But Bert had been thinking.

"I have an idea, Elmo," he said. "Follow me."
Neither of them noticed when a wave of bubbles swept Grover out of the restaurant after them.

Elmo followed Bert up the steps of 123 Sesame Street and into the apartment that Ernie and Bert shared. Elmo laughed happily when he saw inside. It was filled almost to the brim with bubbles! Bert, however, tried to save his paper-clip collection.

Elmo quickly hopped onto a floaty toy that was riding high on the sea of soap.

"Grover! What are you doing here?" Elmo asked when his friend washed in on a wave. "I don't think there are any more floaty toys."

"No problemo," said Grover. "If you can't beat 'em, join 'em." And he started playing a game of catch-the-bubble with a little pink fish.

"Hey! Get back in your bowl, Scadoo," shouted Bert to his pet. But Scadoo seemed happy flipping through the soap.

"Aaargh," Bert grumbled. And he stormed off to the bathroom.

"Hi there, Bert," Ernie said, giving Rubber Duckie a squeeze so that he could squeak hello, too.

"Ernie! I should have known it was you behind this bubble trouble," Bert said. A tide of bubbles wobbled away through the window as he watched. No wonder Sesame Street was covered in suds!

"I guess I *did* leave the water running for a while," said Ernie, blowing a bubble off his nose. "But it took me a long time to find Rubber Duckie. You know I can't take a bath without him."

"Oh, *Ernie*," Bert began, with a thunderous frown. But then his mouth started to curl up into a smile.

Because there was nothing Bert liked better than tidying up, and he suddenly realized that this was going to be a very BIG cleanup job.

"Where's my mop?" he muttered. "I'm definitely going to need my mop. Maybe two."

In the end, Bert needed three, but Sesame Street has never been so clean!

Zoe's Penny

Written by Elizabeth Clasing
Illustrated by DiCicco Studios

There was a shiny-shiny something lying on the sidewalk right in front of 123 Sesame Street.

"Look, Elmo," said Zoe. She swooped down to pick it up. "A penny!"

Elmo told his friend that finding a penny like that was good luck.

"Oh! Here, you have it," said Zoe, holding it out to Elmo. The penny sparkled like a tiny sun in her hand.

But Elmo shook his head. "Finder's keepers! Elmo thinks Zoe should have it."

Elmo followed Zoe home to watch her put the bright new penny into her piggy bank. Zoe's bank was a roly-poly pink pig with a great big smile. Zoe loved putting pennies inside.

Once in a while, Zoe's mommy let her keep coins left over from getting groceries. Sometimes Zoe found pennies tucked into the corners of the couch. And when Zoe was really lucky, she spotted lost ones in unexpected places, like she did today.

Zoe pulled out her piggy bank and tried to drop the penny inside. But this time, the penny refused to go in.

"I'm full!" said the pink pig. Only it wasn't the piggy bank talking—it was Elmo!

"Don't joke me!" Zoe giggled. But Elmo was right. Her piggy was stuffed to the very tippy-top.

"Wow! Zoe could get anything she wants with that many pennies," Elmo said. Then he waved good-bye.

Zoe shook some coins out and started to count. But after eleven pennies, Zoe wasn't sure what came next. Eleventy-two? Zoe needed some help.

She packed up her pennies and went looking for a certain friend. It wasn't long before she found him.

"…28…29…30…31…32!" the Count said. "Thirty-two steps from the corner. Wonderful, wonderful! Ah-aa-aa-ah!"

Zoe covered her ears as thunder went *BOOM* overhead. It always did that when the Count counted something.

Naturally, the Count was happy to help Zoe get past eleven:

"…12…13…14…" the Count said. "Now do you know what comes next?"

Zoe thought hard. "Fifteen!" Together they counted every penny.

"…98…99…100 pennies!" Zoe shouted.

She thanked the Count and rushed to Hooper's Store with her pennies.

Zoe already knew just what she wanted: a pretty bangle bracelet that cost exactly 100 pennies. She was just about to hand over her hundred coins when she spotted something else.

"How many pennies is *that?*" Zoe asked, pointing to a rattle. It was striped in bright colors and made a wonderful *sssh-sssh* sound. Zoe knew someone who would like it *very* much—Natasha, the baby next door. She was so cute and cuddly, and she loved to shake things up!

But Zoe would need 100 pennies for the rattle. And 100 pennies for the bracelet.

"Uh-oh, what should I do?" Zoe wondered. She wished Elmo was there to help her decide.

Zoe thought about how much she liked wearing pretty bangles. Then she thought about Natasha's happy giggle.

After she thought about *both* those things, Zoe turned to the salesmonster, Telly.

"I've decided!" Zoe said with a smile, handing over her hundred pennies.

Later, Zoe knocked on a door in her building. Natasha's daddy, Humphrey, answered.

"I have a present for Natasha," Zoe said, holding out a bag from Hooper's Store.

"*Googaa gubaguba peesh!*" Natasha burbled excitedly when she saw what was inside.

It was a brightly striped rattle.

Zoe felt so happy watching Natasha shake and play with her gift.

Zoe's Penny

"I'm glad you stopped by, Zoe," Humphrey said. He pulled something from the pocket of his coat. "I saw this today and got it for you as a present. You're always so nice to our little Natasha."

In Humphrey's hand was the bangle bracelet from Hooper's Store.

"Oh!" was all Zoe could think of to say. Then, "Thank you sooooo much!"

Zoe hugged Humphrey and gently hugged Natasha, too. Everybody was smiling, but especially Zoe, when she shouted, "What a lucky, lucky day!"

What Do You See, Elmo?

Written by Elizabeth Clasing
Illustrated by DiCicco Studios

On rainy days, Elmo liked to play in puddles. He especially loved jumping in with both feet to make a really big *SPLASH!* But some rainy days were just too drippy for the outdoors.

On days like that, Elmo's mommy let him poke around the shelves in the basement of their apartment building. The shelves were filled with things that people—and monsters—had left behind when they moved or cleaned house.

Today, after playing with a tinny tuba for a while and trying to make a cranky carousel turn round, Elmo noticed something new.

"Elmo doesn't remember seeing *that* before," Elmo said excitedly.

He reached up and pulled it down from its place next to an old ship-in-a-bottle.

"Elmo's never seen anything like this," Elmo said to himself. "But Elmo has *heard* about it before. It's a crystal ball, like the kind they have in fairy tales!"

Elmo thought that maybe he would be able to see something magical inside the crystal ball. He stared down through the dust and, sure enough, seemed to see a blurry picture of himself.

What Do You See, Elmo?

Elmo wasn't sure if the picture was in his head or in the crystal ball, but he didn't care. It was a wonderful picture—Elmo was up on a stage! Elmo was a *star!*

"Look at all the people," Elmo gasped. "Everyone wants to listen to Elmo make music!"

Elmo could hear the *boom-boom* of the drums as Elmo's band played Eensy-Weensy Spider. It was a terrific concert and everyone applauded at the end.

"Thank you! Thank you!" Elmo shouted. He took a bow. Then Elmo giggled at himself. He wasn't on stage at a concert after all. He was in his basement!

"That was fun," Elmo said. "Elmo wants to do that again." He rubbed dust off another patch on the crystal ball and looked inside.

Elmo looked in as swirling clouds filled the ball. They cleared up and Elmo could see something again. This time the picture was different.

"Ooooh, look," Elmo whispered. "Elmo is bigger than an elephant—or ten elephants!"

Elmo imagined what it would be like if Elmo were bigger than even Big Bird, who was the biggest friend Elmo had in the whole world.

Then Elmo wondered, maybe it wasn't that Elmo was *big,* maybe it was Big Bird who got *small.*

"Elmo would take good care of tiny Big Bird," Elmo said. "Elmo would carry Big Bird around Sesame Street inside a flower and ask Zoe if he could live inside her dollhouse."

Elmo giggled at the idea of Big Bird taking Elmo's toy truck for a spin or parachuting down the steps of 123 Sesame Street using a hankie.

"Elmo couldn't call his friend *Big* Bird anymore," Elmo said. He thought a minute. "Elmo would call him Itsy-Bitsy Bird instead!"

Elmo looked in the crystal ball again. Itsy-Bitsy Bird was gone. Instead, Elmo saw something else after the clouds cleared up again.

"It's Elmo!" he said. "And Elmo is even smaller than Itsy-Bitsy Bird! Elmo is as teensy as a flea."

In fact, it was a flea circus inside the crystal ball.

"Elmo's always wanted to be in a circus," Elmo said dreamily. "Elmo will lead the flea-circus parade!"

The fleas would put on shows for all of Elmo's friends on Sesame Street. Every night, at the end of the circus, Elmo and the fleas would ride a toy carousel round and round.

Elmo blinked. There wasn't a picture of a flea circus inside the crystal ball anymore, just a reflection of the toy carousel from the shelf above.

"Oh, Elmoooo!" Elmo heard his mommy call. "The rain stopped and the sun is out. Do you want to go outside and play?"

What Do You See, Elmo?

"Yes!" Elmo yelled back. He put the crystal ball back on a shelf and said, "Elmo will be back on the next rainy day. Who knows what Elmo will see then?"
Do YOU?

THE END